W9-BQL-249

OUT OF
THIS WORLD!

OUT OF THIS WORLD!

Ethan Flask and Professor von Offel
Take on *Space Science*

MAD SCIENCE

by Kathy Burkett
Creative development by Gordon Korman

SCHOLASTIC INC.

New York   Toronto   London   Auckland   Sydney
Mexico City   New Delhi   Hong Kong   Buenos Aires

Bur

0-439-41770-8

The Library of Congress Cataloging-in-Publication Data available

12 11 10 9 8 7 6 5 4 3 2 1   3 4 5 6 7 8/0
                                                          40
Printed in the U.S.A.

Table of Contents

Prologue

For more than 100 years, the Flasks, the town of Arcana's first family of science, have been methodically, precisely, safely, *scientifically* inventing all kinds of things.

For more than 100 years, the von Offels, Arcana's first family of sneaks, have been stealing those inventions.

Where the Flasks are brilliant, rational, and reliable, the von Offels are brilliant, reckless, and ruthless. The nearly fabulous Flasks could have earned themselves a major chapter in the history of science — but at every key moment, there always seemed to be a von Offel on the scene to "borrow" a science notebook, beat a Flask to the punch on a patent, or booby-trap an important experiment. Just take a look at the Flask family tree and then the von Offel clan. Coincidence? Or *evidence*!

Despite being tricked out of fame and fortune by the awful von Offels, the Flasks have doggedly continued their scientific inquiries. The last of the family line, Ethan Flask, is no exception. An outstanding sixth-grade science teacher, he's also conducting studies into animal intelligence and is competing for the Third Millennium Foundation's prestigious Vanguard Teacher Award. Unfortunately, the person who's evaluating Ethan for the award is none other than Professor John von Offel, a.k.a. the original mad scientist, Johannes von Offel. Von Offel needs a Flask to help him regain the body he lost in an explosive experiment many decades ago. So far, his efforts have failed miserably. For example, in *Feed Me! Funky Food Science from Ethan Flask and Professor von Offel*, the professor thought he'd found a nutritious solution to his problem. Unfortunately, what he cooked up was an uncontrollable, supersonic, bouncing *cupcake*!

Now, as Einstein Elementary School prepares for a communications linkup with the astronauts in a space shuttle, the professor is trying to steal a high-tech solution to his out-of-body problem. Will von Offel's space-age shenanigans blast the school into orbit? Or will Mr. Flask's lab assistants expose the professor's ghostly nature before his plan can get off the ground?

The Nearly Fabulous Flasks

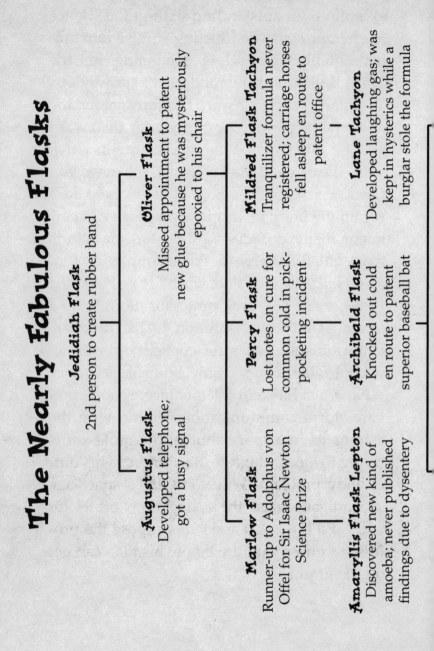

Jedidiah Flask
2nd person to create rubber band

Oliver Flask
Missed appointment to patent new glue because he was mysteriously epoxied to his chair

Augustus Flask
Developed telephone; got a busy signal

Mildred Flask Tachyon
Tranquilizer formula never registered; carriage horses fell asleep en route to patent office

Percy Flask
Lost notes on cure for common cold in pick-pocketing incident

Lane Tachyon
Developed laughing gas; was kept in hysterics while a burglar stole the formula

Archibald Flask
Knocked out cold en route to patent superior baseball bat

Marlow Flask
Runner-up to Adolphus von Offel for Sir Isaac Newton Science Prize

Amaryllis Flask Lepton
Discovered new kind of amoeba; never published findings due to dysentery

Salome Flask Rhombus
Discovered cloud-salting with dry ice; never made it to patent office due to freak downpour

Constance Rhombus Ampère
Lost Marie Curie Award to Beatrice O'Door; voted Miss Congeniality

Solomon Ampère
Bionic horse placed in Kentucky Derby after von Offel entry

Norton Flask
Clubbed with an overcooked meat loaf and robbed of prototype microwave oven

Roland Flask
His new high-speed engine was believed to have powered the getaway car that stole his prototype

Michael Flask
Arrived with gas grill schematic only to find tailgate party outside patent office

Margaret Flask Geiger
Name was mysteriously deleted from registration papers for her undetectable correction fluid

Ethan Flask

The Awful von Offels

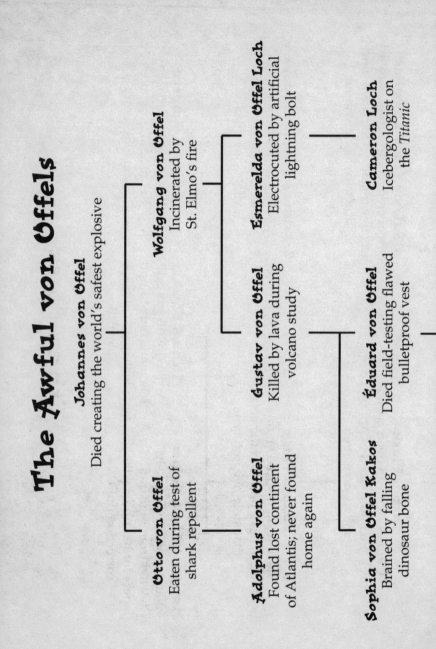

Johannes von Offel
Died creating the world's safest explosive

Wolfgang von Offel
Incinerated by St. Elmo's fire

Esmerelda von Offel Loch
Electrocuted by artificial lightning bolt

Cameron Loch
Icebergologist on the *Titanic*

Otto von Offel
Eaten during test of shark repellent

Gustav von Offel
Killed by lava during volcano study

Éduard von Offel
Died field-testing flawed bulletproof vest

Adolphus von Offel
Found lost continent of Atlantis; never found home again

Sophia von Offel Kakos
Brained by falling dinosaur bone

Rula von Offel Malle
Evaporated

Kurt von Offel
Weak batteries in antigravity backpack

Beatrice Malle O'Door
Drowned pursuing the Loch Ness Monster

Colin von Offel
Transplanted his brain into wildebeest

Felicity von Offel Day
Brained by diving bell during deep-sea exploration

Feldspar O'Door
Died of freezer burn during cryogenics experiment

Alan von Offel
Failed to survive field test of nonpoisonous arsenic

Professor John von Offel (?)

Johannes von Offel's
Book of Scientific Observations, 1891

My scheme to open a gold mine on the Sun is proceeding afoot. There are those in the scientific community who doubt the Sun is covered with gold. They claim it is a flaming ball of gas. Tommyrot! What else but gold could shine so brilliantly? I vow that by year's end I will land, triumphant, upon its glittering surface. (Note to self: Tint monocle dark gray to create a light-ray-blocking "sunglass.") The only obstacle that remains is Earth's gravity. I built a rocket to overcome this irritatingly stubborn force. However, that naysayer, Jedidiah Flask, objected. He claimed its dynamite fuel was dangerous. Naturally, I laughed in his face. Imagine my chagrin, then, when my first attempt blew Flask's greenhouse to smithereens. Flask had the gall to call the authorities. That man has no respect for scientific innovation! No matter. As soon as the court order expires, I will build a larger rocket.

CHAPTER 1

Blast Off with Buzz

Luis Antilla dropped into the auditorium seat next to Alberta Wong and Prescott Forrester. "Any idea why we're here?" he asked.

Prescott looked around nervously. "An emergency school assembly sounds pretty serious. Maybe a teacher has been in an accident? I don't see Mr. Flask."

"I'm sure he's fine," Alberta said.

Boom, boom, boom! On the auditorium stage, PTA president Mrs. Ratner rapped the microphone with a long red fingernail. The lab assistants clapped their hands over their ears. The principal, Dr. Kepler, rushed across the stage to adjust the volume.

Mrs. Ratner leaned into the microphone, her mouth drawn into a frown. "A sprained muscle is a serious thing," she began.

Prescott cringed. "It's Mr. Flask, I just know it."

"It can cause great pain and suffering and even leave permanent damage." The PTA president paused and lowered her head solemnly.

"It must be bad," Prescott whispered. "Poor Mr. Flask."

After a moment, Mrs. Ratner raised her head and flashed the crowd a bright smile. "But it's an ill wind that blows no good. Though we mourn with the rest of the nation that astronaut Tracey Tripp has sprained her thumb, we celebrate that her replacement on this Thursday's shuttle launch will be my cousin Buzz Ratner." She applauded her own news enthusiastically.

Dr. Kepler, and then the puzzled audience, joined in the applause. The principal motioned for the microphone. "We congratulate the Ratner family on Buzz's success!" Dr. Kepler said.

The PTA president leaned toward the mike in the principal's hand. "He'll be the first Ratner in space, but not the last. Right, Joey?"

From the first row, her kindergartner waved uncertainly.

Dr. Kepler smiled politely as she firmly drew the microphone away from the PTA president. "The really exciting news for Einstein Elementary is that Mrs. Ratner and her cousin have been able to arrange a communications link between the shuttle and our school on Friday. There will be a nationally televised session, during which three students will be able to ask Buzz Ratner a question."

Mrs. Ratner reached for the mike. "Students

who are interested in being one of the questioners may stop by the school office this afternoon to pick up an application. Nothing too involved — just a short space quiz and room to write 10 sample questions. Return it to me by tomorrow with three teacher recommendations and a photograph. I'll announce my choices on Wednesday."

"It's no fair," hissed Max Hoof from behind Alberta. "It'll probably come down to you three lab assistants. *I* never get chosen for anything!"

Alberta rolled her eyes.

Onstage, Dr. Kepler was whispering to Mrs. Ratner, who was turning bright red. The PTA president threw up her hands and whispered something urgently back. Dr. Kepler cheerfully shook her head and motioned toward the audience.

"It appears I stand corrected," Mrs. Ratner said, frowning. "The student questioners will be chosen at random and during the broadcast."

Dr. Kepler took the microphone and smiled. "After all, every student here is capable of asking informed, interesting questions. All I ask is that each student have one question ready before the broadcast on Friday."

"Perhaps they could submit them for approval?" Mrs. Ratner said hopefully.

Dr. Kepler shook her head. "We're talking about live television. It's only fair that we keep it spontaneous. Besides, Mr. Flask is gathering materials for the entire school to do an intensive, weeklong study of space. By Friday, each student's head will be bursting with interesting and well-informed space science questions." She handed the mike back to Mrs. Ratner.

The PTA president took a deep breath. "I don't have to tell you that the integrity of the Arcana school system rests on this broadcast. We must all band together to put on a grand show." She shaded her eyes against the stage lights. "Where is Mr. Klumpp?"

The custodian strode to the front of the auditorium and raised his right hand. "Mrs. Ratner, you can count on me to make this school as clean as it has ever been," he vowed.

"I need it cleaner!" the PTA president thundered. "Everyone knows that the TV camera adds an extra 10 pounds of dirt."

Mr. Klumpp nodded and headed for the exit.

"The other PTA parents and I will put together a veritable space festival for Friday," Mrs. Ratner continued. "I see exhibits, special space foods, a Moon walk, and more. Now, students, as you leave the auditorium, I encourage you to imagine yourself *blasting off* into a week of space discovery!"

When the sixth graders arrived for Mr. Flask's science class, the lab was locked.

"Isn't there a rule that if a teacher is more than five minutes late, class is canceled and we get to go home?" Sean Baxter asked.

"That's just a myth," Heather Patterson

scoffed. "I bet you also believe there are alligators in the sewers."

"Whatever," Sean replied. "I'm still setting the timer on my digital watch."

From inside the lab there was the sound of a desk being scraped across the floor.

"Maybe Mr. Flask just forgot to unlock the lab," Alberta said. She knocked on the door.

There was scuffling and another sound of a desk being moved. A full minute later, Professor von Offel opened the door, his parrot, Atom, perched on his shoulder.

"Yes?" the professor demanded.

Sean pushed past him, and the other sixth graders followed suit.

"How did the professor get in here if the door was locked?" Alberta whispered to Prescott and Luis.

"He's a ghost," Prescott whispered back. "It would be nothing for him to sail right through a locked door!"

Luis made a face. "He probably just locked

it himself after sneaking in. You heard him moving things around in here. He was up to something."

Mr. Flask appeared at the door with a huge stack of books under one arm and several bulging grocery bags hanging off the other. "I'm sorry I'm late."

"Four minutes, 38 seconds," Sean said, reading his watch timer. "Are you sure you don't want to step out into the hall for another 22 seconds?"

Mr. Flask laughed. "You don't believe that old story, do you? Anyway, the way we told it when I was in school, once you set foot in the classroom, you have to stay for the whole period whether the teacher shows or not." He set the books and bags on his desk, then looked up, a bit puzzled. "How *did* you get in here, anyway? The door should have been locked."

Atom squawked loudly.

Prescott poked Luis in the ribs. "See?" he whispered.

"The professor let us in," Alberta said.

From his desk at the back of the classroom, the professor cleared his throat. "No need to thank me, Flask. Of course, your tardiness will have to go in my report to the Third Millennium Foundation."

The teacher smiled weakly.

"What's in the grocery bags, Mr. Flask?" Sean asked. "I hope it's salty — or sugary."

"It's both!" Mr. Flask said, a real smile returning to his face. He pulled out a bag of sugar and a canister of salt. "It's the makings of a model solar system. I thought we'd start our space exploration by getting to know our nearest neighbors. Can anyone tell me the planets in our solar system?"

Sean raised his hand. "We had to learn them in fourth grade. I made up a sentence to help us. Remember, Max?"

Max flinched. "Please don't —"

Sean cut him off. "Mommy's Very Eccentric Max Just Showed Us Nosebleeds and Pus."

"A creative but not very classy way of memorizing a list," Mr. Flask said. "Apologies to

Max, and I much prefer 'My Very Extravagant Mother Just Sent Us Ninety Pizzas.' Can you figure that one out, Sean?"

"No sweat," Sean said. "See, the first letter of each word stands for a planet. Mars, no, Mercury, Venus, Earth, Mars, Jupiter, Saturn, Uranus, Neptune, and Pluto!"

"Pluto?" the professor bellowed from the back of the room. Atom, startled, fluttered a few feet into the air. "What rubbish does this school teach children? Clearly, some teacher mixed up his science notes with his classic mythology notes. Pluto is the Roman god of the underworld, not a planet."

The class was silent.

"I've so got him this time," Prescott whispered to Luis and Alberta. His hand shot up in the air.

"Prescott?" Mr. Flask said.

"I just want to make sure I understand the professor correctly," Prescott said, rising to his feet. "It sounds like he's denying the existence of the planet Pluto, which would be very surprising for a modern scientist" — he whirled around and pointed at the professor — "but not at all surprising for a ghost who lived well before Pluto was discovered!"

CHAPTER 2

Pluto Exposed

Alberta buried her face in her hands. Luis sank lower down in his seat. Max scooted his desk a few inches away from the professor.

Sean sneered. "A ghost?" He laughed. "Uh-oh. Ghosts don't like to be discovered. He might come haunt you." He wiggled his fingers menacingly at Prescott.

Max scooted a few more inches away from the professor.

"Sit down, Prescott!" Mr. Flask commanded.

"But —" Prescott protested.

"Now," Mr. Flask said. He sighed. "I apologize, Professor. I'm sure you agree that it's important for kids to have healthy imaginations."

The professor snorted indignantly.

"Of course, we still have to hold them responsible when their imaginations get the best of them," Mr. Flask continued.

Prescott stared stubbornly ahead.

"I think Prescott's embarrassment will be punishment enough when he understands what you meant about Pluto," Mr. Flask said. "Do you want to tell him, Professor? Or should I?"

"This is your classroom," the professor sniffed. "I'll leave the explanations to you."

Mr. Flask nodded. "Prescott, it's not the professor who's behind the times. It's you. Scientists have puzzled over Pluto practically since the day it was discovered, in 1930. The more they learned about it, the less it seemed to fit with the other planets in our solar system. After all, our first four planets are rocky planets. They're medium sized, and their surfaces are, well, hard and rocky. Can someone name them for me again?"

Alberta raised her hand. "Mercury, Venus, Earth, and Mars."

Mr. Flask continued. "The next four planets are gas giants. Just as it sounds, they're huge and they're made mostly of gas. And they would be —"

"Jupiter, Saturn, Uranus, and Neptune," Luis offered.

Mr. Flask nodded. "So, beyond them is Pluto, made of ice and rock, and even smaller than our own moon. Its orbit is much more elliptical than those of the other planets. For years, Pluto seemed like kind of an oddball loner. Then in the 1990s, scientists started detecting other large chunks of ice and rock out in Pluto's part of the solar system. Together, the orbiting chunks formed a huge, wide band, which scientists named the Kuiper Belt. They called the chunks in it Kuiper Belt Objects. They've determined that Pluto is definitely a Kuiper Belt Object, though the largest by far. While Pluto was a puny planet, it's a gargantuan Kuiper Belt Object, about a hundred times larger than the next biggest one."

Alberta raised her hand. "It's like Pluto went from being a little fish in a big pond to being a big fish in a little pond."

Mr. Flask laughed. "Exactly," he agreed.

Luis raised his hand. "Isn't there another belt of huge rocks in our solar system, the asteroid belt?"

Mr. Flask nodded. "That's a big ring of asteroids that lies between the rocky planets and the gas giants. Thousands of them are larger than mountains. And some are even big enough to have their own moons."

"But Mr. Fla-ask!" Max whined. "That's a lot of huge rocks up there. Why don't they crash together, or even crash into Earth?"

"I'm glad you asked that, Max," Mr. Flask

said. He emptied the rest of one grocery sack, pulling out a bag of flour, a box of sugary cereal, a bag of dried peas, and a small cantaloupe.

"Say we shrank the solar system so that the sun was the size of this cantaloupe, about five and a half inches across. How big would Earth be?" the teacher asked.

Alberta raised her hand. "As big as a cherry, maybe?"

Mr. Flask shook his head. "Think smaller."

"A gum ball?" Sean asked.

"Even smaller," Mr. Flask said.

Max pointed to the box of sugary cereal. "Maybe one of those?"

"You're getting closer," Mr. Flask said. He removed two pieces of cereal from the box and set them next to the cantaloupe. "The two largest planets in the solar system, Jupiter and Saturn, would be about a half inch across, like this cereal."

"How about those dried peas?" Heather asked. "Is one of them Earth?"

Mr. Flask removed two peas from the bag and set them next to the cereal. "The other two gas giants, Neptune and Uranus, would be about three eighths of an inch across, like these."

Sean surveyed the other bags of food. "What's left? Sugar crystals?"

Mr. Flask nodded as he opened the bag of sugar. He sifted some crystals between his fingers. "Earth and Venus would be less than a sixteenth of an inch across, about the size of the largest crystals in here." He picked out two crystals and set them on the table.

"Then what's the salt?" Sean asked.

Mr. Flask poured a little salt in his hand and pushed it around on his palm. "The smallest rocky planets, Mercury and Mars, would be less than a thirty-second of an inch across. That's about the size of these two large salt crystals." He placed the two crystals on the table, then reached for the bag of flour. "In comparison, Pluto, the other Kuiper Belt Objects, and the asteroids would be like individual bits of flour — tiny but numerous." He poured a small pile of flour onto his desk.

"I'm going to call you each up here to get one of these planets, or a 'pinch' of asteroids or Kuiper Belt Objects," he continued. "Then I'd like you to spread out until you think you have a scale model of the solar system, one that shows how far away from our cantaloupe Sun these planets would be."

The students crowded around Mr. Flask's desk.

Sean snatched up one of the cereal bits. "I call Saturn! Those rings always remind me of donuts!"

Heather reached for one of the dried peas. "Like Neptune, I'm cool and mysterious."

Max reached for a salt grain, then looked anxiously at the floor. "Mr. Fla-ask! I think I just dropped Mercury!"

Luis dipped his finger in the flour. "I'll volunteer to be the Kuiper Belt."

Prescott ended up with Earth. "Hello, down there," he said.

Alberta held the cantaloupe Sun. The class worked together to line up in the correct order, then moved back and forth to estimate the distance between the planets.

Alberta looked around with a satisfied expression. "See, Max? You don't have to worry about the planets bumping together. There's lots of space between the planets and asteroids and other stuff."

Mr. Flask laughed. "This was kind of a trick assignment, because this room isn't really big enough to fit the solar system at this scale."

"We could go to the gym," Luis suggested.

"Still not big enough!" Mr. Flask opened the door and led the students out into the school yard. He had Alberta stand under one of the science room windows. "Max, now guess how far away Mercury would be at this scale."

"It's not fair!" Max said. "Why does Mercury always have to go first?" He thought for a moment, then stood about three feet away from Alberta and her cantaloupe. He looked up at Mr. Flask.

"Not far enough," Mr. Flask said. "Go back next to Alberta, and take nine good walking steps away from her. That's how far Mercury would be on this scale. Now, Venus?"

"Yo," another student called out.

"You're 16 walking steps away from the Sun. Earth?"

Prescott raised his hand.

"You're 23 walking steps away from the Sun. Now, Mars?"

After a few minutes, the "planets" were spread far apart, with Sean holding his cereal Saturn on the edge of the school yard — a full 214 steps away from Alberta.

"What about Neptune?" Heather shouted across the school yard to Mr. Flask. "Can't I just cross the street?"

"You'd have to go three times as far as Sean," Mr. Flask shouted back. "That's a full 674 steps!" He turned to Luis. "The Kuiper Belt Objects are a bit spread out, but to get Pluto in, you'd have to go 887 steps away."

He motioned for everyone to come back. As

they gathered around him, he said, "Bonus question: How is our solar system different from our model, besides its size?"

Sean looked down at his sugary cereal puff. "It's not vitamin fortified?"

Mr. Flask laughed.

Luis looked around thoughtfully. "The planets aren't usually lined up like this, right?"

Mr. Flask nodded. "It's never happened once in the entire 4.6-billion-year history of the solar system."

Alberta waved her hand in the direction of the school building. "So the solar system would spread out just as far in that direction."

"In *all* directions," Luis amended.

Mr. Flask nodded. "Now, still using our cantaloupe Sun scale, how far do you think Buzz Ratner's space shuttle will be from Earth?"

Sean shrugged and held his hands about two feet apart.

Mr. Flask shook his head, then held out his two index fingers so that they were almost touching. "The distance is so small, you can't really see it on this scale. In fact, enlarge that sugar crystal Earth to the size of a 16-inch beach ball, and the shuttle would only fly between one-quarter inch to one-half inch from its surface."

"That's all?" Sean asked. "Then why even go up there? What can they learn that close to the planet that they couldn't learn back on Earth?"

Mr. Flask smiled. "That sounds like an excellent question for our astronaut linkup." He motioned for everyone to follow him back to class.

As they walked, Alberta heard Sean whispering to Max. "He's gotta be kidding," he said. "If I get called on, I'm not going to waste my question on something like that. I'm going to make broadcast history!"

Mr. Klumpp paced back and forth in his workshop, his arms crossed. "How can I possibly get this school any cleaner?" he said aloud. "I'm already doing everything one man can do. How can I move beyond that?"

He stopped dead in his tracks. "Of course, I can no longer be just one man. To better monitor the school's condition, I'll need eyes in every classroom. Luckily, I've been painstaking in my record keeping." He opened the notebook and paged through a series of classroom maps. "These tell me how much trash and dirt have been left under each desk, almost to the ounce. Using these records, I can identify the tidiest student in each classroom and deputize him or her to be my custodial assistant."

Mr. Klumpp frowned. "I might as well start with the most troubled spot in the building — Flask's classroom." He leafed to a map that was heavily marked with Xs and exclamation marks. "There's hardly a student here who's been left untouched by Flask's love of chaos and disorder." He moved his finger along the rows of desks, shaking his head. Then he stopped short. "Hello. Here's someone I haven't noticed before: Max Hoof. His under-desk rubbish total is impressively low. Well, Max Hoof, you may be just the weapon I need in my war against Flask — that is, *trash*."

After school, Luis, Alberta, and Prescott headed home together. As the last school bus pulled away, a flying wad of paper stung Prescott in the back of the neck. He whirled around to see Sean's head sticking out of a bus window.

"Don't blame me," Sean laughed. "Must have been a ghost!"

The lab assistants walked in silence for a few feet.

"Okay, maybe I shouldn't have tried to expose the professor in front of the whole class," Prescott said finally. "But you *know* I'm right about him. There's no way he knew that Pluto was a Kuiper Belt Object. I mean, this is the man who thought the Internet was something to catch fish with!"

Alberta shrugged. Luis said nothing.

"This isn't over," Prescott said firmly. "I'm going to prove to Mr. Flask that the professor is a ghost, and I'm going to do it *this week*."

Alberta turned to face Prescott. "Are you nuts? Mr. Flask has already made it completely clear that he doesn't believe in ghosts."

"He'll have to if I present him with scientific evidence," Prescott reasoned.

"Like what?" Luis asked. "We went through the professor's desk and office with a fine-tooth comb."

"Don't forget his closet," Alberta added. "I get claustrophobic just thinking about it."

"And none of it turned up any evidence that would convince Mr. Flask," Luis said.

"The only evidence we've ever seen is the professor himself," Alberta added. "We can't exactly capture him and make him walk through another train while Mr. Flask is watching."

"No," Prescott agreed, "but we *can* set up situations that will expose his ghostliness, and then capture it on videotape! I'm sure my parents won't miss their video camera if I borrow it for a few days."

"Are you forgetting what happened when I tried to take photos of the professor?" Alberta asked. "He didn't even show up on the film."

"But his teacup did," Prescott argued.

"Yeah, but that didn't convince Mr. Flask," Alberta said. "He thought it was just a piece of lint on the lens."

"But what if you'd shot a video of the professor sipping tea?" Prescott asked. "The teacup would seem to fly off the table, hover in the air, and float back down again. Mr. Flask couldn't say *that* was a smudge."

Alberta looked at Luis. "What do you think?"

"I don't know," Luis said. "Mr. Flask doesn't seem very open-minded about this. And who can blame him? Six months ago, there's no way I would have believed in ghosts."

Prescott crossed his arms in front of his chest. "I can do this *with* you two, or I can do it by myself."

Luis shook his head. "All right, I'm in. But only to keep you out of trouble."

Alberta nodded. "Me, too. And I'm not sneaking into the professor's yard again."

"There's no need," Prescott smiled. "We can get all the evidence we need at school."

CHAPTER 3

A Perfectly
Normal Question

P rescott carefully lowered his backpack to the floor. "I've got the video camera," he told Luis and Alberta.

"I was afraid you were going to go through with this," Alberta said.

The bell rang. The professor sailed in, with Atom fluttering behind.

"Before we get started," Mr. Flask said, "I want to remind you guys to start thinking of questions for astronaut Buzz Ratner.

"I thought of a question," Sean called out.

"How do astronauts go to the bathroom in space?"

"That's stupid," Heather said. "And gross."

"Think about it," Sean said. "There's no gravity on the space shuttle, right?"

"Very little," Mr. Flask said. "Scientists call it a *microgravity environment*."

"Whatever," Sean said. "So wouldn't anything you put in a toilet float away?"

"Oh." Heather thought for a moment. "Please don't tell me they wear diapers. If Buzz Ratner is wearing a diaper during our satellite hookup, I am going to die."

Mr. Flask laughed. "I can promise that Buzz Ratner won't be wearing a diaper —"

"Good," Heather said.

"— unless we're lucky enough to talk to him while he's outside of the shuttle on a space walk," the teacher continued. "And it's not exactly like a baby's diaper, of course. It's called a urine collection device."

Heather wrinkled her nose. "Couldn't he just hold it until he gets back inside?"

"I'm sure he would try," Mr. Flask said. "But once you're sealed up in a space suit and hanging on the side of the shuttle, it's not so easy to get to a bathroom when nature calls."

"But a diaper?" Sean asked. "That's harsh."

Mr. Flask smiled. "Maybe you'll be the scientist to come up with a better solution."

"Maybe," Sean said. "But first I'll need to know about the space shuttle toilet. I was right about the floating away problem, yes?"

Mr. Flask nodded. "Space shuttle designers had to find something to replace gravity. Their solution was suction."

"Like a vacuum cleaner?" Sean asked. "They 'go' into a vacuum cleaner?"

"Sort of," Mr. Flask said. "Each astronaut has his or her own personal urine cup."

"Well, thank goodness for that," Heather said.

"The urine cup attaches to a hose," Mr. Flask continued. "When an astronaut needs to urinate, he or she just aims into the cup, and the suction pulls the liquid down the hose."

"Do they have another cup, for, you know —" Max asked.

"For solid wastes, they all share one space toilet," Mr. Flask said. "It also replaces gravity with suction. To use it, you would first strap yourself to the seat so that you wouldn't float away. Then you would turn on the suction, and —"

"Fire away!" Sean said.

"So to speak," Mr. Flask said.

Suddenly, Mrs. Ratner stormed in.

"What kind of class are you running here?" she ranted. "I overheard your discussion from the hallway. I can't believe my little Joey goes to a school where children feel free to ask about the — the powder room!"

Mr. Flask took a deep breath. "It's perfectly normal for students to be interested in their bodily functions," he said. "And pondering the effects of microgravity on fluids takes some higher-level thinking skills. I actually thought it was a pretty insightful question."

"Well, here's another insight for you," said

Mrs. Ratner. "If the entire nation sees an Einstein Elementary student ask an astronaut about his 'bodily functions,' our town will be disgraced! Who knows what the ramifications could be?"

"Ramifications?" Mr. Flask asked.

"For one thing, you could lose that prestigious grant you're up for." Mrs. Ratner turned and faced the professor. "Am I right, Professor von Offel? Surely the Third Millennium Foundation wouldn't want to be associated with, if you'll pardon my language, space potties."

The professor stared at her, his expression blank.

She turned back to Mr. Flask and crossed her arms. "Well, even if you don't care what it could do to your career, think of the reputation of our school. I'm sure that all of these children in your class want to go to college someday. Do you really want to jeopardize their chances?"

Mr. Flask drew in a deep breath. "I don't see how —"

"No, clearly, you don't," Mrs. Ratner cut

him off. "Well, let's just hope the rest of our fine teachers see what a potentially explosive situation we have here. And to ensure that they do, I'm going out right now and write a memo!" She turned and stormed out.

In the back of the room, the professor leaned his head toward Atom. "Is it my imagination," he whispered, "or have these people been talking about outhouses?"

Atom rolled his eyes. "Let's remember to schedule a chat about indoor plumbing."

Mr. Flask stood quietly, his eyes on the door.

Alberta raised her hand. "I'm sure we have all kinds of questions."

"Yeah," said Sean. "Like, do they use some kind of high-tech toilet paper?"

"No!" said Alberta. "I mean, like, what does it feel like to be weightless?"

"And what kind of training do you need to be an astronaut?" Luis said.

"Do they eat food?" Heather asked. "Or do they take some kind of vitamin-packed energy pills?"

"And what happens when an astronaut's nose bleeds in space?" Max said.

Alberta groaned.

"It's a valid question!" Max insisted. "After all, there wouldn't be gravity to make the blood drip down."

Mr. Flask smiled. "All of these are great questions. I knew I could count on you guys. Now, let's have a little fun. Here's an activity that can give you the feeling of microgravity without leaving Earth."

"Everybody stand with your side to a classroom wall. Press your shoulder and arm hard against it. Make a fist and press that, too. Ready? Count off 10 seconds, slowly. Now, step away, relax, and . . ."

Sean looked at his floating arm. "Cool!" he said.

After school let out, the lab assistants circled back inside and walked quickly toward the professor's office.

Prescott pulled the video camera out of his

backpack. "Let's start out simple," he said quietly. "The professor often takes a nap after school, yes?"

Alberta nodded. "At least if the snoring sounds that echo through the halls are any indication."

"I'll start the video camera, and you open the door," Prescott said.

"What can you possibly expect to prove with a shot of him sleeping?" Luis asked. "That's *if* he even shows up on videotape."

Prescott shrugged. "We've seen him disappear. We've seen him walk through a train. Who knows what we might catch on tape?"

The lab assistants stopped outside of the professor's office and listened to the rhythmic snoring sounds vibrating through the door.

Prescott held up the video camera. "Lights, camera, action," he whispered. He pressed a button, and the tape began rolling.

Alberta reached for the knob and slowly turned it. She inched the door open. Inside, the professor slumped in his chair, his arms hanging limply and his feet propped up on his desk. Atom slept, too, standing on his perch.

"Ooh, here's an action-packed scene," Luis grumbled.

"Wait, look at the chair seat!" Alberta whispered. "Each time he breathes in, he sinks through the bottom of the seat. You can see his pants hanging below it. Then when he breathes out, he rises up."

"You're right!" Luis said. "Prescott, are you getting this?"

"I'm not sure," Prescott said. "This is an old video camera, and the viewer is really dark. I don't think I'll know until we watch it at home."

"Well, try to get a close-up of the chair seat," Luis urged. "Clearly there's something weird —"

"Awk!" Atom snapped awake. His eyes narrowed at the lab assistants.

"Uh-oh," Luis whispered.

"What?" Prescott asked, his view hidden by the camera.

Atom scrambled off his perch and flew at Prescott, claws first.

An hour later, Prescott was hooking the video camera to the television in his living room. He pressed rewind, then stood up and examined the bruise on his elbow. He shook his head. "I don't understand how something smaller than a chicken dinner could pin me to the ground."

"Well, he did have the element of surprise," Alberta offered.

Prescott pressed play, and the TV screen filled with the image of the professor's office — but no professor.

"I knew he wouldn't show up," Alberta said.

"This was just a trial run," Prescott said. "Anyway, there's Atom. At least we know that *he* shows up on video."

"Awk!" On screen, the image of the parrot got larger and larger, until its feet seemed to strike the inside of the TV screen. The view shifted abruptly, and the camera refocused on the ceiling tiles. Alberta's face poked into view. Her voice played through the TV speakers: "Are you okay, Prescott?"

Prescott stopped the video camera and unplugged it from the television. "Well, it's not much. But at least now we have videotaped evidence that Atom is a dangerous bird."

"Yeah," Luis said. "Along with evidence that we were snooping around the professor's office."

Prescott shrugged and slipped the video camera into his backpack. "There's always tomorrow."

Luis groaned.

CHAPTER 4

A Simple Recipe for Paste

On his way into the science lab the next day, Max stopped in front of the lab assistants' desks. He pointed to a gold-colored star on his shirt.

Alberta leaned forward to read it. "Custodial assistant?"

Max nodded proudly. "Lab assistants may be important here in this classroom, but custodial assistants are responsible for the whole school."

"What do custodial assistants do?" Prescott asked.

The color drained out of Max's face. "Well, they — they assist with custodial things."

"You clean things up?" Luis asked.

"No!" Max said. "At least, I don't think so. We keep an eye on things. We alert Mr. Klumpp to custodial problems."

"You mean big messes?" Alberta said.

Max frowned. "That would be one example. But as Mr. Klumpp says, a custodian's job is much more complicated than just cleaning up spills and emptying garbage."

"What else does he do?" Prescott asked.

"I don't know," Max snapped. "I was only recruited yesterday!" He stomped off.

Sean was coming from the other direction. He took one look at Max's badge and laughed. Sean tipped an imaginary cowboy hat. "Howdy, sheriff!"

Max plopped into his seat and crossed his arms.

Sean wandered up to the front of the science

lab and peered into an open bag of flour on Mr. Flask's desk. The teacher placed a canister of salt next to it.

"Where's the rest of the solar system?" Sean asked. "I could go for a handful of Jupiters and Saturns."

Mr. Flask laughed. "We're going to do a different kind of modeling today. We're going to make landscape models that show the surface features of the rocky planets."

The professor sailed through the door just as the bell rang. Atom followed, veering off in a swift arc right toward Prescott, who was busy leaning over his backpack.

"Duck!" Luis shouted, giving Prescott a quick shove. Prescott toppled to the floor.

"Awk-awk-awk!" Atom lit atop his perch on the professor's desk.

"Doesn't it sound like that bird is laughing at Prescott?" Heather asked.

"What a ridiculous notion!" the professor scoffed. "He could no more do that than sing 'Yankee Doodle Dandy.'"

Prescott pushed himself to his feet. "I'd like to stick a few feathers in *my* hat — and call it justice well served," he grumbled.

"Are you okay, Prescott?" Mr. Flask asked. "Do we need to call in Nurse Daystrom?"

Prescott looked alarmed. "N-no!"

"Okay, then let's get down to work." Mr. Flask handed Prescott the bag of flour and a measuring cup, then placed a large bowl on Prescott's desk. "I'd like you to mix the first batch of modeling clay. Start by pouring three cups of flour into that bowl. Then stir in three cups of salt, followed by two cups of water. While you're working, someone else in your group can choose one of these books to serve as reference for your model."

Max raised his hand. "Mr. Fla-ask! As custodial assistant, I have to protest this potentially messy activity."

"Protest noted, Max," Mr. Flask said. "To keep things a little neater, you can measure out the ingredients for your group."

Prescott tipped his flour bag over the measuring cup. Nothing came out. He tipped it farther. Still nothing.

"Try shaking it a little," Alberta suggested.

Whoosh! An avalanche of flour overfilled the cup and dusted the floor beneath.

"Hey," Prescott whispered to Luis and Alberta. "Remember that meteorite experiment we did that got the flour all over the place?"

Luis nodded. "Are you kidding? I think I inhaled a whole loaf of bread."

"Remember that the professor walked through the flour but didn't leave any footprints?" Prescott said. "We could get him to do that again, and I could get it on videotape!"

Alberta looked nervously over at Mr. Flask, who was helping another lab group. "This doesn't seem like such great timing."

"No time like the present," Prescott insisted. He held the bag of flour over the floor and started lightly coating the aisle with flour.

A few feet away, Max was nervously pouring his second cup of flour into a mixing bowl. He wiped the beads of sweat off his forehead and looked at the floor around his desk. Not a bit of flour spilled! As he surveyed his work area with satisfaction, he heard Alberta's lowered voice.

"Don't you think that's enough flour on the floor?"

Max sprang from his chair. Custodial assistant to the rescue! He ran to the front of his aisle and swung around to face Alberta. She looked nervous. "Where's the flour on the floor?" he demanded.

"What — what do you mean?" she sputtered. She glanced over her shoulder.

Max pushed past her and spotted Prescott. His bag of flour was tipped sideways, and a light dusting of flour was drifting onto the floor. "Not another ounce," Max shouted, grabbing the open edge of the bag. "I'll take that!"

Prescott, startled, tugged back. "Hands off, Max!"

"It's my duty as custodial assistant!" Max

insisted. He tugged harder, putting his weight into it.

Rip! The flour bag tore open, exploding a mushroom-shaped cloud of flour over Prescott and Max.

Max blanched whiter than the flour. "Mr. Fla-ask! I've got to report this mess to Mr. Klumpp!" he shouted. Without waiting for an answer, he rushed out of the classroom.

Prescott calmly brushed the flour off his face and reached into his backpack for his video camera.

"You've got to be joking!" Luis said. "Wouldn't it be better to quit while you're ahead?"

"I can't miss this opportunity," Prescott insisted. He scooted under his desk. "Find some way to get the professor over here!"

"Alberta, is there a problem over there?" Mr. Flask asked from across the room.

Alberta gulped. "No — that is, just a small one." She grabbed a book from Mr. Flask's desk and flipped it open. "We're having some trouble interpreting this map of Mars' surface. Maybe Professor von Offel could help us?"

"Would you, Professor?" Mr. Flask asked.

Atom fluttered from his perch to the professor's shoulder. "It's a trick," he whispered.

"Bah!" Professor von Offel stood up and lumbered down the aisle.

Alberta watched the professor's feet. No tracks! From behind the video camera, Prescott shot her a thumbs-up sign.

"What can I do for you, young lady?" the professor asked impatiently.

Alberta held up the book and pointed to a vast canyon stretching across the surface of Mars. "Um, is this Mariner Trench really a trench? Or is it more of a valley?"

The professor adjusted his monocle and bent over the page. "Hasn't anyone ever taught you what a mariner is, young lady?"

Alberta frowned. "A sailor?"

The professor nodded. "Surely you can work the rest out yourself." He turned on his heel and headed back to his desk.

Luis looked after him. "Can you believe he could say that with a straight face? You've got to admire his nerve, I guess."

Alberta's face reddened. "I think he was just showing us he couldn't be so easily tricked."

Prescott pulled himself to his feet and slipped his video camera into his backpack. "I'd say he was just showing us that he's clueless. He walked through the flour, didn't he?"

Max slammed open the door, bucket in hand. "Nobody move!" he shouted. He raced to the sink, threw the bucket into it, and turned on the tap full blast. "Mr. Klumpp will be here as soon as he can. In the meantime, stay calm, and your custodial assistant will begin the cleaning process." He pulled the full bucket out of the sink and walked toward the lab assistants' desks.

Across the room, Mr. Flask looked up, his arms still covered in flour. "What are you doing, Max?"

At the same moment, Mr. Klumpp appeared at the door, rolling a bin full of mops and brooms.

Max struggled to lift the bucket into view. "Just performing my custodial duties." He tipped the bucket, pouring a thick stream of water onto the flour-covered floor.

"No!" shouted Mr. Flask and Mr. Klumpp in unison.

Max, startled, dropped the bucket and the rest of the water.

Students jumped up on their chairs as the pasty white water rolled across the classroom, leaving lumps of wet flour in its wake. Mr. Flask and Mr. Klumpp rushed to the epicenter of the spill.

Max looked down at his flour-spattered high-tops. "Should I start mopping this up?"

Mr. Klumpp opened his mouth to speak, but only an angry roar came out.

Mr. Flask picked up the bucket. "Perhaps it's time for a unit on chemistry. You wouldn't know this yet, but flour plus water is a simple recipe for *paste*."

Mr. Klumpp finally found words. "My mops and brooms are useless against this!" he stormed. "I have to go back to my workshop and get a flat-tipped shovel!"

Max looked desperate. "Can I help?"

Mr. Klumpp gave him a long, hard look. Then he reached out and yanked the gold star off Max's shirt.

After school, the lab assistants rushed to Prescott's house and connected the video camera to his TV.

Prescott ran the tape. "See? No footprints!"

"Yeah," Luis said. "And no feet, either."

Prescott frowned. "Well, this was just day two. Just wait until tomorrow. Day three's a charm."

CHAPTER 5

Under Pressure

The hall leading to the science lab was blocked by a PTA father with a walkie-talkie in one hand and a bullhorn in the other. "This hallway is closed," his voice boomed through the horn. "Please find another route to your next classroom."

Prescott strained to see around him. "What can they possibly be doing in there?" he said to Luis and Alberta. "Is all this because of the space shuttle hookup tomorrow?" A PTA mother pushed past them, rolling a tire-sized reel of black cable.

The PTA father pointed his bullhorn straight at the lab assistants. "No loitering. I repeat, no loitering."

The lab assistants backed up and circled around toward the science lab. As they passed the principal's office, they saw Dr. Kepler inside, perched on a stool. A hairdresser was draping a smock over her suit as Mrs. Ratner held up a mirror.

"Certainly, your look is appropriate for a principal — very take-charge," the PTA president said. "But you're going to be on TV tomorrow. And a television personality needs a softer and spunkier look."

Dr. Kepler stood up and calmly took off the smock.

"Just give Tanya a chance," Mrs. Ratner pleaded. "I've seen her work wonders with much tougher cases."

Dr. Kepler laughed. "I happen to *like* my hair."

"Thank goodness," Alberta whispered.

In the next hallway, they found Mr. Klumpp on his hands and knees. He ran a toothpick between the floor and the baseboard, then examined the tip closely. He nodded with satisfaction and addressed the passing lab assistants. "Let this be a lesson to you: A hallway is only as clean as its dirtiest crack."

"Um, thanks, Mr. Klumpp," Alberta said. As they turned the next corner, she whispered to Luis and Prescott, "All of the grown-ups here have gone absolutely crazy."

"Maybe," Luis said. "But then Mr. Klumpp didn't have very far to go."

The lab assistants filed into sixth-grade science. Next to Mr. Flask's desk were an eight-foot ladder and three cartons of eggs.

Sean wandered to the front and pulled an egg out of the top carton. "Hey, Max — catch!" He faked a throw as Max dived under his desk. "No wonder you were stripped of your badge," Sean laughed. "A true custodial assistant would have gone for the save."

Mr. Flask took the egg from Sean's hand and motioned for him to sit down. Just as the bell rang, the professor sailed through the open door.

"How does he do that?" Alberta whispered.

Prescott shook his head. "For a man who's been dead for a hundred years, his timing is incredible."

Mr. Flask held up Sean's egg for everyone to see. "Every experiment needs a control, a way to see what would happen without the variable being changed." He climbed to the top of the ladder and held the egg up near the ceiling. "This is our control for today," he said. He let go of the egg.

Splat! The egg shattered on impact, sending arms of sticky egg white across the floor. The broken yolk pooled in the middle.

"No-o-o!" The class turned to see Mr. Klumpp at the door, his mouth hanging open.

Mr. Flask smiled at him reassuringly. "I'll clean it up, of course. Sometimes you just have to make a mess to make a point."

Mr. Klumpp's eyes narrowed. "It's no use even talking to you!" he said to the teacher. He turned to look at Max.

Max shrugged apologetically and pointed to his bare shirt pocket. "I don't have the badge, so I don't have the authority, do I?"

The custodian blew out a noisy breath and stomped away.

Mr. Flask gathered everyone around the splattered egg. "Any ideas on how this tragedy could have been prevented?" he asked.

"Hard-boiling?" Sean asked. "Anyway, I thought we were studying space."

Mr. Flask laughed. "The space shuttle carries a lot of delicate instruments in its cargo bay. If they're not well packaged, the stresses from the flight could turn them into" — he motioned toward the floor — "well, a less sticky but much more expensive mess."

The teacher handed each lab assistant a carton of eggs to pass out. Then he placed some large cardboard boxes on the front desks.

"Your challenge today is to build a container to protect your 'payload' — your egg — from bumps and shocks. You can use any of the materials in these boxes. When perfected, we'll test your container, using an egg and that 10-foot fall."

Max rummaged through one of the boxes and pulled out a large wad of tissues. "At least these will be absorbent if my egg breaks."

"You're starting out all wrong, Max," Heather said. "You've got to plan for success." She examined an empty egg carton. "For instance, this design is already proven to protect eggs."

Sean pulled a bag of marshmallows out of another box. "It doesn't hurt to have a backup plan, though." He ripped open the bag and popped a marshmallow into his mouth. "My test suggests that these are soft enough to cushion my egg. But if they aren't, I can still enjoy a marshmallow omelet."

Alberta picked out half a dozen metal coils.

"The space shuttle is very high tech. I bet I could protect my payload with a complex configuration of springs."

"Maybe," Prescott said, unrolling some bubble wrap. "But sometimes simplest is best."

"Knock, *kno-ock!*" rang out a sugary voice from the doorway. Mrs. Ratner wheeled in a large cabinet. "I've got a very special surprise here, children. After a lot of effort on my part — and Buzz's — I managed to get us this!" Mrs. Ratner swung open the door of the cabinet.

"What is it, a marshmallow suit?" Sean held up a marshmallow and compared it with the white, puffy suit hanging inside the cabinet. "Whoever wears that will be plenty protected."

"That's not candy, dear," Mrs. Ratner said. "It's a *space suit*." She turned to Mr. Flask. "Honestly, four days into your space unit, and one of your sixth graders can't even identify a space suit?"

Mr. Flask laughed. "Sean is our unofficial class clown, Mrs. Ratner. He was joking, but actually he made a very good point. Astronauts on a space walk need even more protection than equipment carried in the shuttle's cargo bay."

"Let's see if it works, Mr. Flask," Sean said. "Put the suit on and jump off the ladder."

Mrs. Ratner's eyes grew wide. She positioned herself between Sean and the space suit.

"Another joke," Mr. Flask assured her. "And naturally that's not the kind of protection I meant. Basically, astronauts have to be protected from space itself. After all, space doesn't have any of the things that our bodies need to survive. Can anyone name some of those things for me?"

The professor sat up straight and looked around at the class.

Luis raised his hand. "Air, water, and food?"

Mr. Flask nodded. "A space suit provides all of those."

The professor's quill moved furiously over his paper.

"But you could get food, water, and air from

a lunch box and a scuba tank," Sean said. "Why wear that big, heavy suit?"

"Great question!" Mr. Flask beamed. "No air in space also means no *air pressure*. That's the pushing force of the air in our atmosphere. We can't feel it, but air puts 14.7 pounds of pressure on each square inch of our skin."

Max slid down in his seat. "I always felt something was weighing me down."

"It seems like it would be fun to have no air pressure," Luis said. "Without that extra weight, you could do some incredible skateboard moves."

"Oh, you wouldn't want to subject your body to no air pressure," Mr. Flask said. "Your body is adapted to that 14.7 pounds of pressure per square inch. If someone were suddenly exposed to an environment with no air pressure, the fluid in their blood would evaporate into gas."

"Boom! They'd explode!" Sean said.

"Well, that's probably overstating it," Mr. Flask said. "Certainly, they'd die pretty quickly.

Scientists predict that the gas in their lungs and intestines would expand rapidly, their bodies would swell and bloat —"

"Ick," Heather said.

"I agree," Mr. Flask said. "And so do space-suit designers. So they pump the suits with oxygen to surround astronauts' bodies with an appropriate amount of air pressure. They have other challenges as well. Out on a space walk, any part of the suit that faces the Sun can heat up to 250 degrees Fahrenheit. Meanwhile, any part in the shade can dip to *minus* 250 degrees. So the inside of the suit has to be well insulated to keep the astronaut from getting too hot *or* too cold."

"And whatever else a regular space suit does," Mrs. Ratner interrupted, "this suit does it even better. It's the EPSSOFF — the Experimental Prototypical Space Suit of Future Flights. It cost $20 million to develop, and it's one of a kind."

"Wow," Alberta said. She reached out a hand to touch the suit's fabric.

Mrs. Ratner quickly swung the cabinet away from her. "No touching, dear. The EPSSOFF is really not even supposed to be out of the laboratory. That's why I promised Buzz that Mr. Flask would treat it with the best of care."

Mr. Flask turned pale. "Me?"

"Who better?" Mrs. Ratner said. "You are the star science teacher here, according to Dr. Kepler. So you should be able to teach the most valuable lesson with it."

Mr. Flask thought for a moment. "Well, the students are certainly interested in it," he said.

Sean stepped forward for a better look. "You say this is a new-and-improved space suit?"

The PTA president nodded. "It's the wave of the future! Maybe someday *you'll* grow up to be an astronaut and wear one of these. Wouldn't that be fun?"

Sean smiled at Mrs. Ratner and pointed to a tube on the front of the suit. "Will this drain away the urine, then? Because they've really got to do something about that diaper-wearing thing before they'll ever get me into one of these suits."

Mrs. Ratner snapped the cabinet door closed and turned toward Mr. Flask. "I've got two dozen parents out there trying to put our best foot forward for Einstein Elementary's national television debut," she fumed. "If one of your students says the word 'urine' while the whole country is watching, I'm holding you personally responsible!" With a last scowl at Sean, she stormed out.

Mr. Flask sighed. "That was really too much, Sean," he said. "Well, why don't you guys get back to protecting your payloads while I figure out how to protect this $20-million space suit."

CHAPTER 6

Not a Perfect Plan

Just before class ended, Prescott pulled Alberta and Luis aside. "I've just developed plan C, but it requires fast action." He pointed to the back of the classroom, where the professor was still writing furiously, his feather quill waving from side to side. "The professor always carries that quill with him between his office and the science lab, right?"

Alberta and Luis nodded.

"I predict that it would show up on film, just like the teacup," Prescott said. "I also predict that he couldn't get it to pass through something solid, like a door. Furthermore, I predict that if the professor can pass through a door, a door could also pass through him."

"Are we supposed to be able to follow this?" Luis asked.

Prescott ignored him. "So here's the plan. As soon as the bell rings, Luis, you run over to the door and hold it open for everyone. But when the professor gets to the door, Alberta, you give Luis a sign. Luis will slam the door."

"What?" Luis said.

"Okay, well, push it closed — hard," Prescott said. "Either way, the door will pass through the professor, knocking the quill to the ground. And I'll get it all on tape."

"Get what on tape?" Alberta asked. "Sounds like you'll capture footage of a feather floating through the air, then being slammed by a door and falling to the ground."

"Well, that's more than we have now,"

Prescott said stubbornly. "Okay, so it's not a perfect plan, but we don't have time to improve it. And we may not get another chance today."

The bell rang. Prescott looked at Luis pleadingly. Luis glanced around for Mr. Flask, who was working with Max and Heather to clean raw egg off the floor.

"Oh, all right," Luis groaned. He took a few quick steps to the door and held it open. Alberta followed, positioning herself just inside the lab. Prescott pulled out his camera and, pretending to examine it, casually pushed the record button.

After most of the students had left, the professor stood up and ambled toward the door, with Atom flying behind. Alberta showed Luis five fingers, then four, then three, silently counting down the seconds until the professor reached the door.

Suddenly, from right behind Alberta, Heather called out, "Sorry I have to go, Mr. Flask. Good luck!"

Alberta tried to signal Luis not to push the door, but it was too late. The door slammed right through the professor — and into Heather's perfect nose.

"Ow!" Heather shouted.

Alberta stood with her mouth open as Mr. Flask and Max came running across the classroom.

"Prescott, go get Nurse Daystrom!" Mr. Flask said. "Alberta, could you get me some tissues?"

Alberta stayed rooted to the spot, staring at Heather.

"Are you okay, Alberta?" Mr. Flask asked. "Did the door hit you, too?"

Alberta quickly shook her head and turned to find the tissue box.

Mr. Flask and Max looked at Heather's nose.

"It doesn't *look* broken," Mr. Flask began. He took a handful of tissues from Alberta and handed them to Heather.

"I think it's just a bloody nose," Max said.

"And I should know. Just pinch your nostrils, lean forward, and —"

The door swung open, and the professor wandered back in. "Did I leave my quill somewhere around here?" he asked.

Max picked up the feather off the ground and handed it to him. Then something else caught his eye. "Hey, what's that?" he asked, pointing.

The professor cocked his head. "Why, that looks like Atom." He scooped up the stunned bird, who had ricocheted off the closing door and been knocked halfway across the room. "Now, how did that happen?" he murmured as he wandered back into the hallway.

A moment later, Nurse Daystrom rushed into the room, followed by Prescott and a very sheepish Luis.

"Are you okay?" Luis asked.

Heather nodded. "I just don't understand what happened."

The nurse examined Heather's nose. "Max's diagnosis was right, and so was his recommended treatment." She smiled at Max approvingly.

Max blushed. "I was just passing along what you've taught me over the years."

Nurse Daystrom helped Heather to her feet. "Max, could you help me get our patient to the nurse's station?" she asked. "I bet you could find it with your eyes closed."

"Sometimes I do, just for the fun of it," Max said. "After all, it's sometimes hard to see when you're dealing with a nosebleed."

Down the hall, Professor von Offel sat in his office, sifting through his notes from the science lab. Atom was sprawled on the floor with his scaly feet poking up toward the ceiling.

"Space study is so invigorating," the professor said. "I definitely picked the right time to come back to life — I can see the stars in my future!"

"I can see stars in my present," Atom moaned. "Can't somebody make them stop spinning?"

The professor frowned. "Buck up. It was only a door. Or are you getting soft on me?"

"I may be soft," Atom said, "but unlike you, I'm also *solid*. You have no idea how much it hurts to be hit by a door. And why should you? Your body just passes through to the other side."

The professor held up his stack of notes. "Well, that will soon be a thing of the past. I've finally found the tool that can return me to full corporeality."

With a grunt, Atom rolled to his feet and fluttered up to the desktop. He glanced over the professor's notes. "That $20 million space suit?" he squawked. "How in the world could *it* help restore you to life?"

"As Flask pointed out, the EPSSOFF provides air, food, water, air pressure, and a stable temperature — everything a body needs for survival," the professor said.

"Yeah, but before you can *survive*, you first have to be alive," Atom countered.

"Listen and learn," the professor said. "With the EPSSOFF, survival is guaranteed at the medium settings. As you point out, that's inadequate for my needs. So it follows that I should explore the suit's high settings. I'm confident that if I crank every knob up high enough, I'll provide myself with enough life-giving elements to restore my missing 35 percent."

Atom shook his head. "I've got a brain the size of a walnut. Do I really have to be the one to explain the flaws in that logic?"

The professor opened his top drawer and shoved in the stack of notes. "If naysayers like you had their way," he said gruffly, "scientists would never fulfill their dream to someday land on the Moon."

Atom opened his beak to speak, then shut it again.

"And even more tragically," the professor continued, "I'd never find a way to steal that space suit."

※ ※ ※

After school, the lab assistants watched Prescott's video footage in silence. The image on the screen was crisp and clear: The professor's quill seemed to magically levitate off his desk. The camera followed it as it flew unsteadily through the air. Luis flashed into the frame as he gave the door a shove. The feather hit the door and fell. A second later, Heather crumpled to the floor in pain.

Luis pushed the eject button, pried the ribbon of tape out of the cassette, and calmly tore it to shreds.

Prescott didn't say a word.

CHAPTER 7

How to Stalk a Wild Professor

On Friday, Einstein Elementary was decked out like a carnival. Students milled around the school yard, checking out a huge model space shuttle made by fifth graders or lining up at space-themed game booths.

"That Welcome Astronauts banner is so big, they could practically see it from space," Luis said.

"Look, a Moon walk!" Alberta said. "When I was little, I loved to bound around inside one of those, pretending I was an astronaut."

Prescott wrestled the video camera out of his backpack. "This is perfect," he said. "With all this commotion going on, I won't have to sneak around with my camera. I'll just pretend I'm documenting this historic occasion. All the while, I'll be collecting evidence against the professor."

Luis's body stiffened. Alberta watched his expression darken, then she turned to Prescott. "Don't you think we should give it a rest after what happened yesterday?" she said. "Maybe it's not so important that we prove the professor is a ghost."

Prescott glanced over at Luis. "Look, I'm sorry that Heather got hurt, and I know it was my fault. But like I said at the beginning, I'm dedicated to doing this, with or without you."

"Well, you'll definitely have to do it without me," Luis said.

Alberta bit her lower lip. "Maybe if we wait

and talk about this on Monday we'll have a better perspective on things."

Prescott shook his head. "No, I think I'm seeing things very clearly right now. Catch you guys later, I guess."

Alberta watched as Prescott wove himself into the crowd of students. "I think we hurt his feelings," she said.

"Better his feelings than his nose," Luis replied.

Inside the science lab, Mr. Flask was studying a set of scratches around the lock on his closet door. "That's odd, these almost look like claw marks." He walked along the counter at the back of the classroom and stopped at the third cage. He peered in at a mole that was curled up in the corner. It lifted its head sleepily. "You're the only one here with claws that sharp," the teacher said. "But your cage is shut tight — and anyway, how could you get up there?" He scanned the other cages. "Who here is a good climber?"

Suddenly, the teacher laughed. "Right, an animal is going to try to open the closet and steal the space suit. Clearly I've been working a little too hard on this space shuttle linkup." He walked back and unlocked the closet. Then he pulled out the cabinet and opened its door. "Well, whatever made those marks, the EPSSOFF is safe. And in just about an hour, Mrs. Ratner will wheel this suit away, and I'll gladly lose $20 million worth of worry." He rolled the cabinet out of the lab and headed toward the auditorium.

He arrived just as the television crew was finishing its last equipment check.

"Hey, buddy," one of the workers said. "You going to be here for the next half hour?"

Mr. Flask nodded. "You bet."

"We've got to go get lunch," the worker said. "I wouldn't normally leave our equipment, but we're shorthanded here. And this seems like a nice, safe little town."

"I'll keep an eye on things," Mr. Flask assured him.

The worker paused at the door. "See that large screen on the stage? It alone is worth thousands of dollars."

"Hmmm, impressive," Mr. Flask said, pushing his $20-million load up a ramp to the stage. He stopped and wiped the sweat off his hands. "You guys enjoy lunch. Everything will be safe."

He positioned the cabinet on the stage and opened its door. He paused to look at the suit's high-tech fabric. Mrs. Ratner had asked the students not to handle it, but he was the teacher, after all. Just a quick touch, he decided, a brief, physical connection with the future of space travel. He reached out a finger and gently ran it along the sleeve.

"Mr. Flask!" Mrs. Ratner screeched.

The teacher started and spun around. "Y-yes?"

"There's no time to lose! We're due to be interviewed on the school lawn in eight minutes!"

"What?" Mr. Flask said. "Don't you need me to guard the EPSSOFF?"

"I need you outside even more," Mrs. Rat-ner replied. "The TV news shows want a teacher, and you're the best I've got."

"But I also promised the TV crew I'd look after their stuff." Mr. Flask motioned to the cameras, screens, and cables.

Mrs. Ratner waved his protest away. "Their stuff is peanuts compared to the value of the EPSSOFF."

"But isn't that even more reason why we need someone here?"

"The show starts in seven minutes now! Just close the cabinet. Then you can lock the door to the auditorium; we'll be back in a few minutes, anyhow."

"Maybe I could wheel the suit back to the lab closet," Mr. Flask reasoned. "Then on the way back, I could snag someone to watch the TV equipment."

"There's no time!" Mrs. Ratner said. "This is live television. We simply *can't* be late. As it is, I just have time to drop by the teachers' lounge and check my hair."

Mr. Flask reluctantly closed the cabinet. Then he followed the PTA president out of the auditorium, locking the door behind him. "Sorry, guys," he said quietly. "I'll try to be back before your lunch break is over."

Outside, some of the sixth graders sat together, eating their special "space lunch."

"This astronaut ice cream is delicious," said Sean, finishing off the freeze-dried treat. "It's crunchy like a cheese puff, but sweet, too. Those fresh carrots made my stomach a little queasy, though. So where's our special space toilet?"

"Gross," Heather said. "Haven't we heard enough about that?"

Sean laughed. "I can't wait until the hookup," he said. "If my name is called, you know what I'm going to ask about."

"We've got to warn Mr. Flask," Alberta whispered to Luis. "You heard Mrs. Ratner say she'd hold him responsible if anyone asked about space toilets."

Luis shrugged. "The whole school is here. That makes Sean's chances of being chosen, like everyone else's, less than one in 300."

"Just in case, though, shouldn't we have a plan?" Alberta said.

"What do you have in mind?" Luis asked warily.

"Well, if his name is called, I'll keep him in his seat. You stand up and pretend to be Sean. It's not like Buzz Ratner or the television crew is going to know the difference."

"No offense, but do you really think you can hold Sean down? He's a lot bigger than you."

"Okay, so it's not a perfect plan," Alberta said.

"Uh-oh," Luis said. "Where have I heard *that* before?"

"Well, there's less than a one in 300 chance we'll even have to try it," Alberta argued. "I'm open to any other suggestions."

"All right," Luis said. "But if we see Prescott, let's recruit him to sit on the other side of Sean. He owes me one after that door job."

Meanwhile, Prescott was across the school yard, pretending to take video footage of the line for the Moon walk. He panned over the waving students, but he was really searching the crowd behind it for Professor von Offel.

"Where is he?" Prescott muttered to himself. "Everyone is supposed to be out of the building until the big hookup." He stopped the video camera and made a face. "Of course, when was the last time the professor followed the rules?" Prescott circled behind the Moon walk and slipped around the corner to the back of the school building. He found the deserted rear entrance, and with a quick glance behind him, ducked inside.

He peeked around the corner and down the hallway toward the science lab. Sure enough, the professor and Atom were at the classroom door. The professor was busy jiggling the knob. Prescott aimed his camcorder and pushed record.

"Why would Flask lock his classroom?" the professor said. "The man trusts nobody."

"Warn me if you decide to walk through the — *AWK!*" Atom fluttered up and away, just as the professor took an impulsive step through the door.

A moment later, the professor pushed open the door and stepped back out into the hallway, frowning. "The suit is gone. Things would be much easier right now if you'd just gotten that closet lock open last night."

"Well, I couldn't concentrate with all of those beady eyes watching me," Atom said.

"You're blaming Flask's classroom pets for your failure?"

Atom bristled. "What other explanation is there? Under normal circumstances, I've never met a lock I couldn't pick."

The professor grunted. "Where could Flask have taken my space suit?"

"Maybe he took it to the auditorium for the space shuttle hookup," Atom suggested.

"No, he's more likely taken it to the auditorium for that rocket show they're having.

Come, there's no time to lose." The professor stormed off down the hall.

Atom followed with a sigh.

Prescott waited until they got around the corner, then took off running in the opposite direction. He wound his way through the building and got to the auditorium before the professor and Atom. The door was locked, so he slipped into a closet across the hall and poked his camera lens out of the door.

Almost immediately, the professor flashed by. He walked straight through the auditorium door without stopping to see whether it was locked. A minute later, he pushed open the door, carrying the space suit in a bear hug. "Now would be a good time for you to earn some of that bird seed you wolf down," he said to Atom. "This thing weighs a ton!"

Atom grabbed the space suit by a tube and pulled. Together, bird and man wrestled the suit back to the science lab. Prescott followed carefully behind, camera rolling.

Moments later, Mr. Flask returned to the auditorium. He was surprised to find the door unlocked, but a quick glance proved that the TV equipment was all in place and the EPSSOFF cabinet stood on the stage, right where he'd left it. He felt an itching urge to check inside the cabinet. It seemed silly, but he was about to do it anyway when a long line of kindergartners marched in, led by Dr. Kepler.

"Wonderful! Mr. Flask can help direct you to your seats," she told the students. "I'm going to go get the first graders."

Mr. Flask glanced anxiously at the cabinet, then laughed at himself. What could have possibly happened to the EPSSOFF in those short 10 minutes? He turned to help the kindergartners.

In another 10 minutes, the auditorium was full. Dr. Kepler quieted the crowd. Then Mrs. Ratner held up a large fishbowl. "In this bowl are the names of all of our students," she announced. "When the time comes for the astronaut questions, I'll choose names from this bowl. Think very hard about your questions. Everyone in the nation — including your parents — will be watching."

"That's overstating it a bit, isn't it?" Alberta whispered to Luis.

On her other side, Sean was softly chanting, "Pick me, pick me, pick me, pick me. . . ."

Luis craned his neck to look around the auditorium. "When was the last time you saw Prescott?" he asked Alberta. "He's not here."

"I don't see the professor, either," Alberta said. "Wherever he is, Prescott must be following him."

Luis nodded. "That explains it. I hope he gets the footage he wants."

"But what if the professor catches Prescott filming him?" Alberta said. "He might do anything to keep his secret. Prescott could be in big trouble!"

Luis looked past Alberta at Sean. "I guess I'm willing to go look for Prescott. But are you sure you want to leave the other matter to chance?"

Alberta turned toward Sean. He had his fingers crossed and he was whispering, "Space toilets, space toilets, space toilets . . ."

She turned back to Luis. "Let's go looking for Prescott *right* after the shuttle linkup is over, okay?"

CHAPTER 8

Crank It!

Halfway across the corridor, Prescott was crouched in front of the science lab. He had managed to push the door slightly open, and he was filming through the crack.

Inside, the professor was clomping around the room, wearing the bottom half of the space suit, which looked like white, puffy pants with attached boots. "Not very dapper," he said. "But styles do change."

The top half of the suit lay facedown on Mr. Flask's desk. "Hold her steady!" Professor von Offel ordered. Atom landed on the top of the suit. The professor positioned his arms over his head, took a few running steps, and dived into it. Atom flapped his wings to help pull it on. Then the parrot pulled a formfitting cap over the professor's head and fastened it under his chin. The professor placed the helmet over his head, and Atom locked it to the suit. Then Atom carried over the two gloves and attached them to the end of each arm.

Atom perched on the professor's shoulder and started punching buttons and turning dials with his beak. The suit's life-support systems whirred and clicked as they turned on. Atom looked at the suit's gauges. "I feel like I'm forgetting something."

The professor pointed at his helmet, then began gesturing wildly.

"Oh, the microphone," Atom said. He flipped a switch with his claw.

"Right now, you birdbrained, beak-faced, feather-headed —"

"You're coming in loud and clear," Atom interrupted.

"Oh, so I am," the professor said. "Well, follow me."

Prescott scrambled behind as the professor swung the door open. After the pair disappeared around a corner, Prescott slipped into the science lab. He opened a series of supply closets until he found what he wanted. Then, tucking a half-full bag of flour under his arm, he took off after the professor and Atom.

On the large screen, Buzz Ratner's smiling face hovered over the whole student body.

Meanwhile, Mrs. Ratner's frowning face hovered over the fishbowl. She squeezed her eyes shut, thrust in her hand, and pulled out a slip of paper. "Hayley Bopp," she announced to the darkened auditorium.

The TV crew focused the spotlight on a

blond third grader. "Do you think humans will ever build a colony on Mars?" she asked.

"I hope so, Hayley," Buzz said. "Let me tell you why."

Mrs. Ratner relaxed a little.

"This is a historic moment. I don't intend to spend it in Flask's classroom." The professor's voice sounded tinny over the space suit's microphone. He panted with the effort of moving the heavy suit across the deserted school yard.

"That would be a lot more private, though," Atom pointed out. "For someone who's just stolen a $20-million piece of equipment, you don't seem too concerned about being caught."

"I'm a scientist," the professor replied. "I have a right to borrow scientific equipment. In fact, I have an obligation!"

"Let me see if I follow you," Atom said. "You're saying that ripping off this space suit was the only moral thing you could do?"

"Naturally!" The professor stopped in front of the Moon walk. "According to the sign, this is some kind of lunar simulator. To get the full effect of this space suit, a low-gravity environment might help."

"Low gravity?" Atom said. "No, see, that's just a children's ride. The kids bounce up and down and —"

"I wouldn't expect you to understand the scientific principles involved," the professor snapped. "Just lift that flap, and help me inside."

Atom clamped onto the canvas door with his beak and tugged hard. The heavy fabric barely budged.

"Put some muscle into it!" the professor urged. "Don't you realize that I'm standing in plain sight wearing a stolen space suit?"

The canvas dropped out of Atom's beak. "And you'll be that much less noticeable when you're bouncing around the Moon walk?"

The professor gripped Atom with a huge white glove and pushed his way into the Moon walk. He took a few small, experimental jumps. "Not quite what I expected of the Moon's surface," he said. "But very intriguing."

Mrs. Ratner shut her eyes and reached into the fishbowl for the second time. She swirled the slips of paper around for a few seconds, before coming up with one. She opened it expectantly, but then her face turned pale. She showed the name to Dr. Kepler and gestured toward the fishbowl: Could she choose again? The principal shook her head. Mrs. Ratner's voice trembled as she read, "Sean Baxter."

In the back of the darkened auditorium, there was a loud laugh, then a shuffling sound. Luis stood up and blinked into the spotlight. Behind him, blocked from the camera's view, Alberta was holding Sean down by pure force of will.

"Hey," someone said, "that's not —"

Luis cut her off. "We've been studying space suits this week, and I was wondering: Do you

have any suggestions for space-suit designers?"

"Give us a way to scratch an itchy nose!"
Buzz laughed. "Seriously, the main job of a
space suit is to keep you alive in the hostile environment of space. Anything on top of that is
just icing on the cake."

Prescott scrambled from tree to tree, getting
ever closer to the Moon walk. He held the
video camera in one hand and still clutched
the bag of flour in the other.

Inside the ride, Atom adjusted the dials on
the front of the suit.

"Higher!" The professor gestured upward
with both thumbs.

"But some of these gauges are already in the
hazardous zone," Atom told him. "You don't
want to lose that 65 percent corporeality that
you still have, do you?"

"In for a penny, in for a pound!" the professor urged. "Higher!"

Atom cranked the dials higher. The space suit began to expand with the increasing pressure inside.

Back in the auditorium, Mrs. Ratner reached into the bowl one last time and pulled out a slip of paper. Her forehead glistened with nervous sweat. She took a deep breath, unfolded the paper, and then smiled broadly. She showed the name to Dr. Kepler. The principal looked surprised, but she nodded.

"By coincidence," Mrs. Ratner said to the image of Buzz Ratner, "our last question comes from your little cousin, Joey Ratner."

There were a few disappointed grunts as Joey stood up.

Outside, Prescott watched in horror as the EPSSOFF expanded to twice its usual girth. The professor, immobilized, toppled over and bounced to a halt.

Atom tried desperately to push his way out

of the Moon walk exit, but the canvas door was too heavy for him.

Joey stared at the screen in silence.

"Go on, dear," Mrs. Ratner encouraged.

Finally, Joey opened his mouth. "Cousin Buzz, how do you go to the bathroom in —"

BOOM! An explosion drowned out the rest of Joey's words and rocked the auditorium.

Mrs. Ratner jumped to the microphone. "Luckily — I mean, unfortunately — there seems to be some kind of emergency on this end. We'll have to forgo that last question." With the push of a button, she cut the shuttle link.

Prescott, temporarily deafened by the exploding space suit, followed Professor von Offel's trajectory with his video camera. Ribbons of fabric from the shredded suit and the Moon walk fell all around him, but Prescott kept the camera on von Offel.

The professor finally landed, after a few bounces. Prescott stepped out from behind a tree. Still filming, he walked to the professor's side. "Are you all right, Professor?"

Professor von Offel sat up and scowled. "Of course I am. Why wouldn't I be?" A bedraggled Atom landed on his shoulder.

"I just saw you fall about 50 feet," Prescott said.

"Nonsense," the professor said. "Poppycock. What is that thing in front of your face?"

"It's a video camera," Prescott said. "You're busted, and so's your bigmouthed bird."

The professor turned to Atom. "Is this true?"

Atom laughed. "I bet he can't prove anything. You don't show up in mirrors. Why would you show up on a videotape?"

Poooof! Keeping the video camera steady, Prescott pulled his arm from behind his back and tossed the flour bag. Man and bird were covered with flour. As the white powder coated the professor's face, his features were clearly outlined for the camera. "Even if your body flying through the air doesn't show up on tape, your flour-covered face will," Prescott said. "It will look like you suddenly appeared out of nowhere. I call that documentary proof that you're a ghost." With a satisfied grin, Prescott turned off his camera and walked toward the school. Halfway to the building, Alberta and Luis met him.

After school, the lab assistants reviewed Prescott's footage.

"Wow," Alberta said. "Can't argue with that proof."

Prescott smiled broadly. "I told you I'd get it."

"Yep," Luis agreed. "Mr. Flask and Dr. Kepler won't be able to dismiss this evidence. As soon as they see this footage, they'll have to throw the professor out of school and contact the Third Millennium Foundation."

Prescott's smile faded.

"I'm sure the foundation will send a replacement as soon as possible," Alberta assured him. "You're doing them a favor, really, by bringing a dishonest evaluator to light."

Prescott shook his head. "Oh, no. What was I thinking? The last thing the Third Millennium Foundation will want is for everyone to know that one of their representatives was a conniving ghost! That will make the foundation people look ridiculous for not checking out von Offel thoroughly. They'll just want the whole thing to die down quietly. Mr. Flask will *never* win the Vanguard Teacher Award now. Why did I ever make that tape?"

"Well, you don't *have* to show it to anyone else," Luis said quietly.

"But after all that Prescott went through?" Alberta asked.

Luis looked at Prescott.

Prescott sighed. "I guess we should keep it a secret — for now."

"If we ever really need the proof, though, you'll have it," Alberta said. "And since the professor *knows* you have it, maybe he'll be on better behavior."

Across town, at the von Offel mansion, the professor was pounding on a table. "It's too much to bear — a Flask taking credit for my scientific discovery! It was so devious of him."

"So von Offel-like," Atom said.

"Precisely," the professor said. "No Flask has any business acting that way."

"He was only taking responsibility for the destruction of that $20-million suit," Atom argued. "I thought it was a pretty noble act — very Flask-like."

The professor sniffed. "It may have been Flask-like at first. But then what did he do when they started thanking him for discovering a fatal flaw in the space suit's design?"

"What could he do?" Atom asked. "He had no proof regarding who stole the suit and blew it up. Of course, I imagine he had his suspicions."

"That should have been enough for him to give me the credit," the professor insisted. "That's been the problem with all of the Flasks. They always wait for proof."

"Speaking of proof, I'm a little worried about Flask's lab assistants," Atom said. "What do you think they'll do with their video evidence?"

"Absolutely nothing," the professor chuckled. "I've got them over a barrel. They won't risk losing the Vanguard Teacher Award for their precious Mr. Flask. So what can they do?"

"How about turn you in, sell the videotape to a television producer, and retire at age 12?" Atom said. "They'd earn enough dough to fund a thousand teacher grants, resod that hole you put in the school lawn, and maybe even replace that high-tech space suit. . . ."

Welcome to the World of
MAD SCIENCE!

The Mad Science Group has been providing live, interactive, exciting science experiences for children throughout the world for more than 12 years. Our goal is to provide children with fun, entertaining, and exciting activities that instill a clearer understanding of what science is really about and how it affects the world around them. Founded in Montreal, Canada, we currently have 125 locations throughout the world.

Our commitment to science education is demonstrated throughout this imaginative series that mixes hilarious fiction with factual information to show how science plays an important role in our daily lives.

To discover more about Mad Science and how to bring our interactive science experience to your home or school, check out our website:

http://www.madscience.org

We spark the imagination and curiosity of children everywhere!